SAMURAI SANTA

A Very Ninja Christmas

To Sander, Fred, and Ash

Ultra awesome thanks: Laurie Klaass
Super-uber mega thanks: Kristin Ostby and Chloë Foglia
Thank you too, Gerron Lamson

SIMON & SCHUSTER BOOKS FOR YOUNG READERS
An imprint of Simon & Schuster Children's Publishing Division
1230 Avenue of the Americas, New York, New York 10020
Copyright © 2015 by Rubin Pingk
All rights reserved, including the right of reproduction in whole or in part in any form.
SIMON & SCHUSTER BOOKS FOR YOUNG READERS is a trademark of Simon & Schuster, Inc.
For information about special discounts for bulk purchases, please contact Simon & Schuster Special Sales at
1-866-506-1949 or business@simonandschuster.com.
The Simon & Schuster Speakers Bureau can bring authors to your live event. For more information or to book
an event, contact the Simon & Schuster Speakers Bureau at 1-866-248-3049 or visit our website at
www.simonspeakers.com.
The text for this book is set in Prova.
The illustrations for this book are rendered digitally.
Manufactured in China
0816 SCP
10 9 8 7 6 5 4 3 2
CIP data for this book is available from the Library of Congress.
ISBN 978-1-4814-3057-9
ISBN 978-1-4814-3058-6 (eBook)

SAMURAI SANTA

A Very Ninja Christmas

By Rubin Pingk

Simon & Schuster Books for Young Readers
New York London Toronto Sydney New Delhi

Christmas Eve was the most **PERFECT** snow day of the year.

Yukio had never seen such **BIG** snowflakes.

They seemed full of magic.

Yukio dressed for the snow
and went outside,
where he found himself
ALONE.

He needed more ninjas for an **EPIC** snowball fight.

"NO!"

the rope-climbing ninjas replied. "**SANTA** wants us to be good little ninjas."

"NO!"

said the balancing ninjas. "**GOOD** little ninjas practice their skills."

"NO!"

said a sword-fighting ninja.

"We don't want to be on Santa's **NAUGHTY** list."

Yukio felt **SAD** and **LONELY**.

"It's Santa's fault nobody will play.

SANTA must be chased away!"

Yukio was upset.
He didn't care about presents
or stockings or even lumps of coal.

SANTA
was in the way of
a good snowball fight.

So Yukio

PLOTTED

to run Santa
out of Ninja Village.

All the **GOOD** little ninjas were asleep,

but not Yukio.

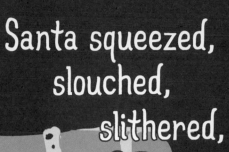

Santa squeezed,
slouched,
slithered,

and stumbled
DOWN
the chimney . . .

to surprise

SANTA.

Yukio crept to the **LOUDEST** gong around.

CRASH!

"INTRUDER!"
Yukio shouted.

"Everyone
WAKE UP!"

Sleepy ninjas **CHASED** the bright red intruder.

Who WAS he?

They could not find him
ANYWHERE.

Suddenly a

SAMURAI

stood on the hill with an
army of snowmen.

They
TUMBLED
in the foothills.

Snow
ZOOMED
across housetops.

Snow **FLEW** through the trees.

the samurai was NOWHERE to be found.

Then Yukio realized:
His friends would have **NO** presents from Santa,

and it was all HIS **FAULT!**